VISIT US AT
www.abdopublishing.com

Published by ABDO Publishing Company, 8000 West 78th Street, Edina, Minnesota 55439.

Copyright © 2010 by Abdo Consulting Group, Inc. International copyrights reserved in all countries. No part of this book may be reproduced in any form without written permission from the publisher. Buddy Books™ is a trademark and logo of ABDO Publishing Company.

Printed in the United States of America, North Mankato, Minnesota.
112009
012010

PRINTED ON RECYCLED PAPER

Coordinating Series Editor: Rochelle Baltzer
Editor: Sarah Tieck
Contributing Editors: Heidi M.D. Elston, Megan M. Gunderson, BreAnn Rumsch, Marcia Zappa
Graphic Design: Deborah Coldiron, Maria Hosley
Cover Photograph: *iStockphoto*: ©iStockphoto/geotrac, ©iStockphoto/Rouzes; *Peter Arnold, Inc.*: R. Andrew Odum.
Interior Photographs/Illustrations: *Eighth Street Studio* (pp. 7, 17, 24, 30); *Essence Animals CD*: Ingram Publishing (p. 15); *iStockphoto*: ©iStockphoto/Birdimages (p. 20), ©iStockphoto/carebott (p. 29), ©iStockphoto/Cay-Uwe (p. 20), ©iStockphoto/cglade (p. 29), ©iStockphoto/ChuckSchvaPhotography (p. 7), ©iStockphoto/foxalbot (p. 10), ©iStockphoto/gbrundin (p. 9), ©iStockphoto/gkuchera (p. 29), ©iStockphoto/hartcreations (p. 19), ©iStockphoto/mammamaart (p. 29), ©iStockphoto/rocketegg (p. 23), ©iStockphoto/rusm (p. 19), ©iStockphoto/Themalx (p. 25); *National Park Service*: Sally King (p. 5); *Peter Arnold, Inc.*: ©BiosPhoto/Gunther Michel (p. 17), John Cancalosi (p. 13), R. Andrew Odum (p. 5); *Photo Researchers, Inc.*: Gregory G. Dimijian (p. 27), Dr. Morley Read (p. 15); *Shutterstock*: Sz. Akos (p. 25), James Coleman (p. 5), Geoffrey Kuchera (p. 10), m.p.imageart (p. 5), smeya (p. 5), worldswildlifewonders (p. 9).

Library of Congress Cataloging-in-Publication Data

Murray, Julie, 1969-
  Disgusting animals / Julie Murray.
    p. cm. -- (That's wild! : a look at animals)
  ISBN 978-1-60453-977-6
  1. Animal behavior--Juvenile literature. 2. Animal defenses--Juvenile literature. I. Title.
  QL751.5.M87 2009
  590--dc22
                                2009033006

Contents

Wildly Disgusting! 4
Playing Possum 6
Skunk'd! 8
Nice to See You 12
Hoot Hoot 14
Want Some Dinner? 16
Birdie Bites 18
Clean Up 22
Do I Know You? 26
That WAS Wild! 28
Wow! Is That TRUE? 30
Important Words 31
Web Sites 31
Index 32

Wildly Disgusting!

Many amazing animals live in our world. Some are big and others are small. They may fly, run, or swim.

Some animals are wildly disgusting! They have habits that are totally gross. But, these yucky habits are often important for their survival. Let's learn more about disgusting animals!

Horned Lizard

Pacific Ocean

Skunk

Playing Possum

Opossums can play dead for up to six hours at a time!

Opossums just want to be left alone. These **marsupials** live in dark dens. When something frightens them, they hiss and show their teeth. If that doesn't work, they play dead.

Opossums go into a deep sleep when they play dead. A stinky goo comes out of their rear. Some people say it smells like a rotting body.

Stay Away!
Opossums have about 50 very sharp teeth.

7

Skunk'd!

Can you think of another animal that uses smell to **protect** itself? How about the skunk?

It's easy to recognize a skunk's unusual black-and-white fur. But, you can smell skunks even when you can't see them. Their stinky spray leaves behind a terrible odor. It smells so bad that it helps keep predators away!

Skunks are small. Yet, their strong smell protects them from enemies.

Skunk spray is oily and hard to remove. Taking baths in tomato juice may help get rid of it.

A skunk can spray as far as ten feet (3 m).

Special body parts called glands produce a skunk's spray. Two small glands are beneath the tail. When a skunk feels scared, yellowish liquid sprays out from these glands.

Skunks often give a warning before they spray. Some raise their tails and stomp their feet. Others hiss. One type even does a handstand! Such signs mean a skunk is getting ready to spray. Look out!

Science Shows...
Skunk spray can come out in a mist or a stream.

Nice to See You

Other animals **protect** themselves in different ways. Horned lizards do not move very fast. Their spiky scales match their surroundings. This helps keep them safe.

When that's not enough, the horned lizard has another trick. It **squirts** blood from its eyes! Usually, this confuses or scares away predators.

A horned lizard can squirt its blood as far as several feet!

Hoot Hoot

An owl can turn its head nearly all the way around!

Animals can have some pretty disgusting eating habits. Owls aren't picky eaters. They eat squirrels, mice, worms, and other creatures. If their meal is small enough, they don't chew it. Instead, they swallow it whole!

An owl's body uses all the **nutrients** it can. But fur, bones, and teeth can't be **digested**. So, the owl **regurgitates** these parts.

What an owl regurgitates is called an owl pellet. People take apart owl pellets to learn what owls eat.

Want Some Dinner?

A jackal pup sometimes licks its mom's or dad's mouth when it wants to eat.

Jackals are **scavengers**. That is gross enough! But, there's more.

Jackal parents feed their young by **regurgitating**. After they throw up their food, their pups eat it. Jackals do this every few hours so their pups don't go hungry.

Yummy! Koalas, birds, and other animals also feed their young by throwing up.

It Burns!
Vulture vomit is strong enough to burn skin! That's because vultures have a lot of acid in their stomachs. This lets them eat dead animals without getting sick.

Birdie Bites

Some animals use puke to **protect** themselves. When a vulture thinks it may be attacked, it throws up on its enemy. Vultures mostly eat dead animals. So, their stinky barf is full of **digested** bits of those. Just the smell can scare off a predator!

Vultures are often looking for their next meal. Sometimes they even wait around for animals to die.

Most vultures do not have feathers on their heads. This helps them stay clean while eating rotting dead animals.

Vultures have good uses for their **urine**, too. When they are hot, they pee on themselves. This cools down their bodies. And, vulture urine is strong enough to kill bacteria. Sometimes, vultures pee on themselves to keep clean.

Bald eagles eat vulture puke. Ick!

Clean Up

Giraffes have very talented, useful tongues. A giraffe sticks its tongue deep into its nose to clean it! At about 20 inches (50 cm) long, its tongue can go far. A giraffe also uses its tongue to catch bugs on its face and eat them. Eeeeww!

A giraffe uses its tongue like a hand or a finger.

High Point
Giraffes are the tallest animals. Males can be 18 feet (5 m) tall!

Thick, slimy spit coats a giraffe's long tongue. Wherever it licks, it leaves behind a gooey trail! The spit coats thorns or sharp plant parts. This **protects** the giraffe when it eats those types of plants.

Giraffes eat leaves and other parts of tall trees.

A giraffe's tongue is dark blue. This may help keep it from getting sunburned.

Do I Know You?

Naked mole rats live in colonies in underground tunnels. They can't see well. So, they smell their way around.

Colony members go to the bathroom in the same spot. They roll around in this area so they all smell the same. That way, they know who is a friend and who is an enemy.

Naked mole rats eat their poop too! This gives them extra **nutrients**.

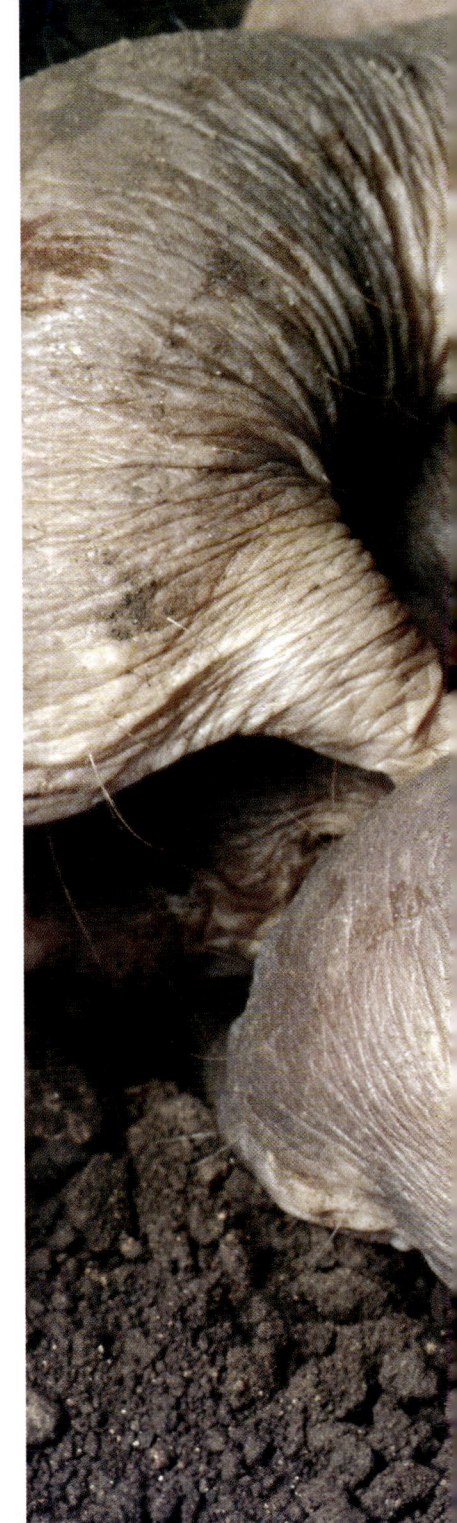

Naked mole rats have droopy, pinkish skin and big front teeth.

That WAS Wild!

From puking vultures to **scavenging** jackals, there are some very disgusting wild animals. Each of them is an important part of the animal kingdom.

People work hard to **protect** animals and their surroundings. You can help, too! Recycling and using less water are two simple things you can do. The more you learn, the more you can do to help keep animals safe.

It is important to reduce, reuse, and recycle. This helps protect areas where wild animals live.

Observe an animal home, such as a bird's nest, instead of touching it. That way, the animal won't be scared away.

Several types of owls are at risk in certain areas. Their homes are disappearing as cities grow. So, some people make nesting boxes where owls can live.

Wow! Is That TRUE?

🐾 The grass cows eat causes gas to build up in their stomachs. There's so much that it leaks out. So, cows burp and fart a lot!

🐾 Hagfish are covered in a slimy goo. If attacked, some can make enough slime to fill a whole bucket in just one minute! This helps them slip away from attackers.

🐾 When a fly lands on your food, it spits on it. This breaks down the food. Then, the fly sucks it up!

Important Words

digest to break down food into parts small enough for the body to use.

marsupial (mahr-SOO-pee-uhl) a kind of mammal. Female marsupials usually have a special pouch for carrying young.

nutrient (NOO-tree-uhnt) something found in food that living beings take in for growth and development.

protect (pruh-TEHKT) to guard against harm or danger.

regurgitate (ree-GUHR-juh-tayt) to bring back up from the stomach.

scavenger (SKA-vuhn-juhr) an animal that eats garbage or dead animals it did not kill.

squirt (SKWUHRT) to shoot out in a thin stream.

urine (YUHR-uhn) a clear, yellowish liquid that is made by the kidneys and released from the body as waste. It is also called pee.

Web Sites

To learn more about disgusting animals, visit ABDO Publishing Company online. Web sites about disgusting animals are featured on our Book Links page. These links are routinely monitored and updated to provide the most current information available.

www.abdopublishing.com

Index

animal homes **6, 26, 29**

bald eagle **21**

conservation **28, 29**

cow **30**

defense **6, 8, 11, 12, 13, 18, 30**

eating habits **14, 15, 16, 17, 18, 19, 21, 22, 24, 25, 26, 28, 30**

enemies **8, 12, 18, 26, 30**

fly **30**

giraffe **5, 22, 23, 24, 25**

hagfish **30**

horned lizard **4, 12, 13**

jackal **5, 16, 28**

koala **17**

naked mole rat **5, 26, 27**

opossum **6, 7**

owl **14, 15, 29**

skunk **4, 8, 9, 11**

vulture **18, 19, 21, 28**